Drop It, Rocket!

To Jill Parker
and Nancy McKay,
who helped me learn
how to read

 Published in the United States by Schwartz & Wade Books,
an imprint of Random House Children's Books, a division of Random House LLC,
a Penguin Random House Company, New York.
Schwartz & Wade Books, and the colophon are
registered trademarks of Random House LLC.
Visit us on the Web!
randomhouse.com/kids
Educators and librarians, for a variety of teaching tools, visit us at
RHTeachersLibrarians.com
Library of Congress Cataloging-in-Publication Data
Hills, Tad.
Drop it, Rocket / Tad Hills.
pages cm
Summary: "Rocket loves to collect words for his word tree with his teacher, the little
yellow bird. Watch as the pup finds new words like leaf, hat, star, boot, and many more"
—Provided by publisher.
ISBN 978-0-385-37247-3 (hardback) — ISBN 978-0-385-37248-0 (glb)
ISBN 978-0-385-37249-7 (ebook) — ISBN 978-0-385-37254-1 (pbk.)
[1. Vocabulary—Fiction. 2. Dogs—Fiction. 3. Birds—Fiction.] I. Title.
PZ7.H563737Dr 2014
[E]—dc23
2013041866
The illustrations in this book were rendered in colored pencils and acrylic paint.
Manufactured in China
10 9 8 7 6 5 4 3 2 1
This book has been officially leveled by using the F & P Text Level Gradient™ Leveling System.

Drop It, Rocket!

by Tad Hills

schwartz & wade books • new york

Rocket and
the little yellow bird
love words.

They love
their word tree,
too.

“Are you ready
to find new words
for our word tree?”
asks the bird.

"Yes, I am!"
says Rocket.

Rocket finds a leaf.

"Drop it, Rocket,"

says the bird.

Rocket drops the leaf.

He is a good dog.

Rocket finds a hat.

"Drop it, Rocket."

Rocket drops the hat.

"Good boy."

Rocket finds a star.

"Drop it, Rocket."

Rocket drops the star.

"Good boy."

Rocket finds a red boot.

"Drop it, Rocket,"
says the bird.

“Drop it, Rocket.”

“Drop it, Rocket.”

Rocket likes the boot.

He will not drop it.

“Will you drop it
for a ball?”
asks the bird.

Rocket will not drop it.

“Will you drop it
for a stick?”
asks Emma.

Rocket will not drop it.

“Will you drop it
for a sock?”
asks Fred.

Rocket will not drop it.

"I have an idea!"
says Owl.

Owl finds a book.

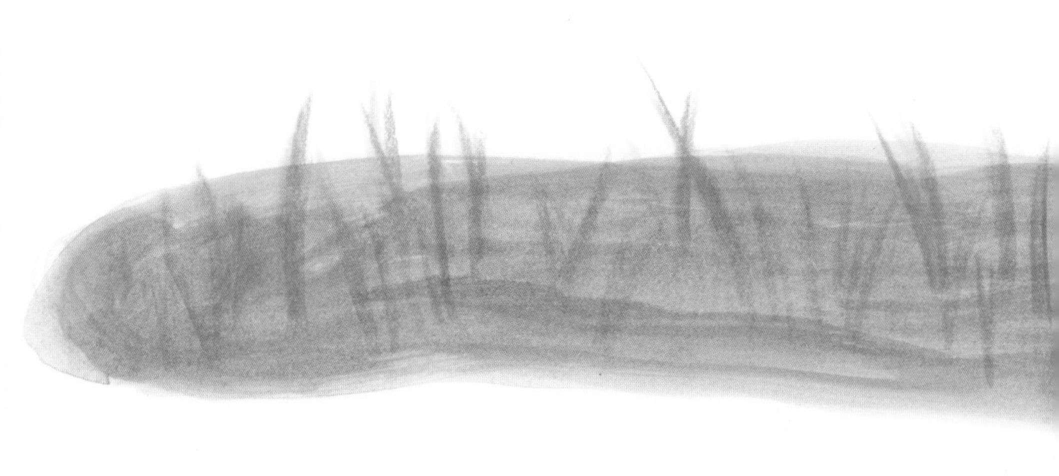

“Will you drop it
for a book?”
asks Owl.

Rocket drops the boot.

"Rocket dropped it!"
says the bird.

Rocket is a good dog.

star
tree
leaf
dog
bird
book
boot
sock
stick
hat